HALE-MANO
A Legend of Hawai'i

HALE-MANO

Retold by David Guard

Illustrations by Caridad Sumile

La'ie-'ula
Hau-'ula
Ko'olau Range — Kua-loa
Kaha-Lu'u
Maka-pu'u
Hale-mano
Wai-a-lua
Wai-anae Range
O'AHU

KAUA'I

NI'IHAU

A Legend of Hawai'i

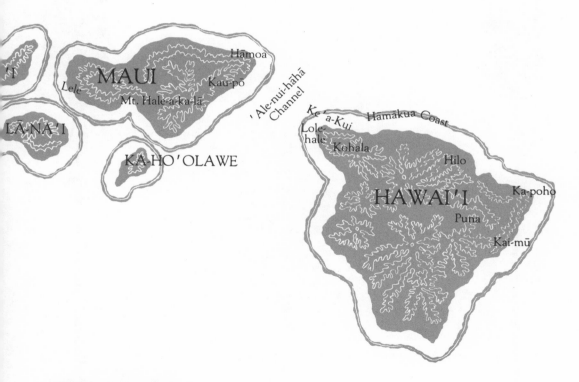

TRICYCLE PRESS

Berkeley, California

TRICYCLE PRESS
P.O. Box 7123
Berkeley, CA 94707

The Library of Congress has catalogued an earlier edition as follows:

Guard, David, 1934–1992
    Hale-mano.

    Bibliography: p.88.
    SUMMARY: Retells the legend of Hale-mano, a young man who abandons all activities to search for his true love, Princess Kama.

    1. Hale-mano (Legendary character)—Juvenile literature.
[1. Hale-mano (Legendary character) 2. Folklore—Hawaii]
I. Sumile, Caridad. II. Title.
PZ8.1.G93Hal   398.2'1'09969   80-69773
ISBN 0-89742-048-9 AACR1

First published by Celestial Arts, 1981
First Tricycle Press printing, 1993
ISBN 1-883672-04-X

Manufactured in the United States of America.

1 2 3 4 5 – 97 96 95 94 93

Introduction

The legend of Hale-mano comes to us from the long years before Ka-mehameha made all the Hawaiian Islands his kingdom in 1794 — how long before, no one can say. The ancient storytellers kept the memory of Hale-mano's adventures vigorously alive in the spoken literature of Hawai'i. Then in the 1860s and '70s Judge Abraham Fornander employed a group of eminent Hawaiian folklorists, among them S. N. Ka-makau, S. Hale-ole, and Kepelino Ke'au-o-kalani, to collect and write down a great number of the surviving legends. Some results of their search appeared in Hawaiian language newspapers of the day. The whole collection of manuscripts was published with English translations between 1917 and 1919 by the Bishop Museum of Polynesian Ethnology and Natural History in Honolulu.

Several short English language variations have appeared since that time, both in print and over the airwaves, while the original Hawaiian verses remain as popular as ever and are often requested of the chanters at the *hula* festivals of today.

1

The present version arises from the desire of its designers (both natives of Oʻahu) to provide a well-rounded entertainment. It may also serve the needs of those who wish to follow in the footsteps of the narrative while visiting the Islands.

We wholeheartedly recommend the sources listed in the bibliography; we lingered long over them, and our obligation to the archivists is enormous. On the other hand we never hesitated to draw upon our own experiences of Hawaiian life. Above all we send our thanks and our love to the people of Old Hawaiʻi and their children.

Aloha kākou,
David Guard and
Caridad Sumile

The Hawaiian Alphabet

a, e, h, i, k, l, m, n, o, p, u, w

Unstressed Vowels:
a = like *a* in alone
e = like *e* in set
i = like *y* in study
o = like *o* in rose
u = like *oo* in spoon

Stressed Vowels:
ā = like *a* in father
ē = like *ay* in stay
ī = like *ee* in sweet
ō = like *o* in over
ū = like *oo* in spoon

Glottal Stop:
' = like the English oh-oh
(in Hawaiian: 'o'o)

Consonants:
w is sounded as *v* after i or e
t is used in imported words

This happened a long time ago in Old Hawai'i. . . .

On the island of O'ahu there was a young man called Hale-mano, and that name means 'many houses.' You can start at Wai-a-lua on the northwestern shore and follow the Hale-mano stream inland across the red slopes of the Wai'anae Range to the place where Hale-mano was born. There were many houses up there in those days.

He was the youngest of six children, and his grandmother took good care of him until he had grown up straight and strong, with clear skin and friendly eyes. He was very handsome and able to finish anything he started, but now Hale-mano was caught in the net of his dreams.

Every night, instead of enjoying restful sleep, he had a vision of a lovely girl who came and spoke to him; she would tell him her name in the dream, and from the very first he was deep, deeply in love with her. But every morning when he woke, he could not remember her name or any of the words that had passed between them. Hale-mano was in such a condition that he could think of nothing else but this girl. He lost all interest in the world around him and would not even eat or drink. Awake or asleep he was always trying to find some way to reach her. He became very ill, and his family watched him sadly as he kept losing weight.

They wished that his oldest sister would return home. Her name was Laenihi, and she was born with many gifts of magic and healing. Laenihi had been traveling around the islands taking care of people with her mysterious powers, but in a very short while she appeared at her brother's bedside and was now bending close to his ear.

"I saw your face in the clouds and heard your voice on the wind calling me to come. How did you get into so much trouble?"

Hale-mano was too sick to make any answer, and Laenihi saw that she had to start healing him right away. She prepared an oven and covered it with five sheets of *tapa* cloth; and then she baked a red hen in it, to be presented as an offering to Hi'i-aka, the goddess of medicine. And, laying the sacrifice before her on an altar of stones, Laenihi chanted this prayer:

> "O Hi'i-aka, spread forth your love over my brother.
> Pardon his sins and impurities,
> His errors in worship, the faults of his heart,
> His careless words, his unkept promises.
> May your anger be removed by this offering.

8

Look with favor on him,
Bring him prosperity all his life,
Keep his body healthy until he has
Passed the time of walking upright,
Until he shall crawl or walk bent over a staff,
Until he shall be blink-eyed then bedridden.
Keep him healthy until the last trance-vision.
O Hi'i-aka, that is your blessing to us
And thus I worship you."

After this she made a hut called a *hale hau* because it was built with sticks of *hau* wood, and this was arched on top. She had her sick brother carried into this little hut, where she had prepared a steam bath for him. After his illness had steamed away she cooled him with sea water, rubbed his scalp with coconut oil, and gave him red *taro* juice to drink. Then she wrapped a scarf around his shoulders and covered his body with *maile* ferns and ginger branches. He was sleeping dreamlessly at last.

The next morning, while the rays of dawn were growing to a full flaming pathway of sunrise, Hale-mano remembered that he had been gazing for some time at the dazzling appearance of the healing woman. Although he recognized his sister, he rubbed his eyes and sat up to make sure he was not still tangled in sleep.

Laenihi asked him again how he had come so near dying.

"It's because I cannot stop dreaming about this perfect girl. The only chance I get to meet her is in my sleep. Every night she comes over, and we go walking and talking under the trees, or go surfing together in the big waves. We're always together all night long, but every morning she disappears and I have to start dreaming all over again to be with her. I'm trying to find out who she is and where she goes every day."

"Tell me what she looks like," said Laenihi.

"Well, she is tall and very lovely," Hale-mano said. "Her eyes and body are wonderful. She has long, straight black hair. She's very dignified and behaves like the daughter of a chief."

"Now tell me how she dresses when you see her in your dreams," said Laenihi.

"Her dress seems to be made of some beautifully scented *tapa*, and her *pā'ū*, her skirt, is made of some very light material dyed red. She always wears a creamy white *hala* wreath on her head and a *lei* of bright red *lehua* flowers around her neck."

10

Laenihi was finding this very interesting. She said to her brother, "On Hawai'i, the Big Island, you find *lehua* blossoming in the districts of Hilo and Puna. In Puna you find the famous scented *tapas* of 'Ola'a. In Puna you see them wearing the *noni*-dyed red *tapas*. I think your loved one must live in Puna; she doesn't come from the west. Don't worry, I know I will be able to help you. But first you have to tell me how your meetings come about."

"Just after I fall asleep, she comes and tells me her name; but whenever I wake up, I forget it."

"Does she come to you every time you go to sleep?"

"Yes. Even now you could hear us talking if I went to sleep."

"Then sleep, Hale-mano," said his wise sister, "and I shall watch over you. When you meet your loved one, ask her to tell you her name and where she comes from."

With a sigh, the young man closed his eyes and the sadness left his face. Then his lips began to move as if he were talking with someone, but the words were very soft.

His sister bent nearer to listen. She heard him whispering, "Kama . . . Puna . . . Ka-poho . . ."

Laenihi saw that her brother's face was full of joy. Shortly after this she woke Hale-mano from his dream.

"The girl's name is Kama," said Laenihi, "and I have heard much about her. Her parents are chieftains over the land of Ka-poho. She is famous for her beauty—far superior to all the women of Puna. But she is being brought up under very strict *kapu*. She lives in her own house and has only her young brother for a friend. When she comes of age, she will be given in marriage to either the king of Puna or the king of Hilo. They both have been sending her valuable presents, and making gifts of property every year to her parents as well. However, the Princess Kama has never met either one of these kings."

Hale-mano was jumping with excitement. He shouted, "I want to marry her myself! Kama doesn't have to live alone or marry anybody else! I'm going over there and bring her back to O'ahu with me!"

Laenihi looked at him fondly and said, "You had better eat and get your strength back first if you expect to take her away from those powerful kings. And, while you are regaining your health, I will pay this Princess Kama a visit to find out if she is really the girl you have been dreaming about all this time."

Hale-mano completely trusted his sister, and her words filled his heart to the brim with hope. He promised that he would eat well and take the best care of himself while she was away.

Before Laenihi left for the Big Island she told her family of the signs she would show so that they might be able to follow her travels.

"If it pours rain here, you will know that I have gone as far as the island of Moloka'i. If lightning flashes very hot, then I am at the island of Maui. If it thunders in a deep voice, you will know I have reached Kohala, the northwest part of the island of Hawai'i. If an earthquake shakes you, then I am at Hāmākua, the northeast part of Hawai'i. And if overflows stain the streams red, you can be sure that I will have gone all the way to Puna, where the princess lives. All these signs I have told you, you should fix firmly in your mind or else you will forget."

She laughed quietly to herself, because she had not really told her family everything she was about to do . . .

Laenihi went down to the seashore at Wai'anae and made a prayer to Hika Po Loa, the One Power that is in everything, that she might take the form of a fish. Next she entered a sacred *kupua* trance in which her life energy was brought to a standstill, and during this time she was completely absorbed and intermingled with the Divine Power. Then she came back into being as the labroid fish, which is known by the name *Laenihi* right up to the present day. And that evening, small and colorful, she splashed into the sea on her mission.

She was going by the southwest coast of Moloka'i, and it began to rain back on O'ahu. Her family was astonished at the great speed she was traveling. From there she passed off the south coast of Maui, and the lightning flashed. The people were surprised, quick-as-a-flash. Leaving Maui behind, she swam the waters of 'Umi at Kohala on Hawai'i, and the roar of thunder was heard. Farther on, as she sped by the Hāmākua coast, they felt the shock of an earthquake. From there past Hilo, going by Pana-'ewa and on to Ku-kulu outside Puna, the red rainwater ran. When this happened, the people behind were sure that Princess Kama would be found.

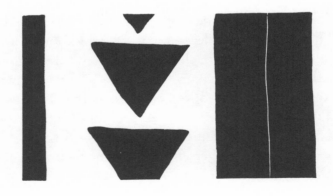

When Laenihi reached Puna she immediately started on her plan to meet the princess, who was never allowed to mingle with anyone but her own family. Laenihi figured that, if she were ever going to speak with her, it would have to be inside Kama's house and at a time when no one would be looking to find them.

Her strategy was complete. Laenihi willed for the sea wind to blow, which woke the ocean from its flat calm and sent a big surf rolling in to Kai-mū beach. People have always gone to Kai-mū for the great surfing there, and early on this morning the blue, powerful swells were beginning to stand up far from the shoreline.

People rose from their sleep and started shouting when they realized the size and shape of these waves. They ran for their surfboards and got ready to ride.

Kumu-kahi was the young brother of Princess Kama. He heard the roar of the voices above the crash of the surf, and he was very excited. He ran from the beach to Kama's house to beg her to let him use her surfboard.

"Kama, the waves are perfect!" shouted Kumu-kahi. "Come on, I'll help you carry the board!"

"I know why you want to help carry," she laughed. "Well, let me ride a few first to make sure the current isn't too swift for you."

Kama loved her brother so much that she never could refuse him any request, large or small; so they picked up the surfboard between them and trotted out to the special part of the beach reserved for their family.

When they reached the surf line, Kama stood on the black sand and waited for the chance to take her board out between the coming of the waves. She let the first rough, grinding pounder go by. The second, soupy white wave was filled with seaweed stirred up by the first, and she allowed this to pass also. Then came the third and largest of the set, like the tooth of some gigantic whale; and when it had spent its force on the shore she saw there would be a short period of calmer water. She plunged in and paddled her board out just beyond the first break.

As soon as she got clear, she spun around and dug in ahead of the first bright swell that came along. She handled its tremendous power as lightly as she would a feather and, standing with great poise, she guided the board right back into the shallows near the beach.

She went sliding on the waves three more times and was becoming more and more delighted with her sport, when suddenly the wind died down and the surf disappeared. Kama waited patiently offshore for the breakers to build up again; but after a long time, dejected and stiff from the cold, she decided to head for home. As she was pulling back into shallow water, she noticed her brother jumping up and down on the beach and calling to her.

"Look at that bright fish! Look, right there by your board! Get the fish! Catch it for me!"

Kama looked down and saw the fish very near her and hardly moving at all, just below the sparkling surface of the water. She reached over and gently surprised the fish, cupped it up and folded it into her skirt, and then paddled in to where Kumu-kahi was eagerly waiting.

The fish was Laenihi, of course, but they had no way of knowing that. While Kama kept her wetted down with seawater, Kumu-kahi ran to get a wooden calabash to keep her in. He returned shortly, and they started off for home with the new plaything in the bowl.

This is the way Laenihi was able to come into the house that was forbidden to everyone except the princess and her brother. The house was covered in vines, with two *kapu* staves standing beside the entrance to warn intruders that a high-ranking family lived there under royal protection.

In the middle of the night after everyone had fallen asleep, Laenihi changed back into her form as a woman and came and stood where the princess lay. Kama woke and saw the stranger looking at her.

Laenihi was quite startling in appearance, all wet from the sea. Her skirt was a *pā'ū* spangled with crystals, and over her shoulders hung a short mantle the colors of a rainbow. Her long hair was held back by a *lei* of flowers, and her wrists and ankles were adorned with tiny pink and white shells.

Kama asked her, "Where do you come from?"

"I am from near here," Laenihi replied.

"There is no woman who is like you anywhere near. Besides, no one belonging to this place would come into this house because they all know that it is *kapu*—forbidden to enter on the pain of death."

Laenihi told her, "I have come from far away, beyond the sea."

"Yes, now you are telling me the truth," said Kama.

Laenihi then began to speak about why she had come. She asked the princess if she ever met a young man in her dreams. Kama would make no answer to this, so Laenihi tried another question:

"Would you let me have some old wreath of yours, one that's withered and worn out?"

"I do have an old wreath like that, but I can't give it to you. It's full of *mana*, my spirit, and if I let you take it away you might use it to cast a spell on me."

Laenihi told her, "It's all right, you can safely give it to me. If you ever become ill, you can call to me; and, because I have something of yours, I will be able to work through it to cure you. I am living at Kai-mū. They call me the sight-seeing woman."

Hearing these kind words, Kama was glad to give her the withered wreath and one of her scented dresses as well. The two new friends talked well into the night but, when it was time to think of safety, Laenihi vanished into the shadows before they were again pierced by the long rays of dawn.

Laenihi went back to her brother.

"It's good to see you strong and healthy again," she said, "because we will soon be sailing to Puna on the Big Island. I got the chance to meet the beautiful Princess Kama of your dreams. She was very happy to hear about you, and she wanted you to see these things."

And Laenihi showed him the wreath and the scented *pā'ū* that Kama had given her.

"Come, let's go to Puna!" Hale-mano said urgently. "I just can't wait to see her!" You have to show me how to get there!"

"No, not right away," Laenihi told him. "You will not be able to win her unless your plans are very well prepared; so there are certain things to do before we go. We must make some nice toys for Kama's younger brother. I have noticed that whatever he wants, she gives him. She never denies him any request; so if we take something along with us that he wants, he will send his sister to get it from us. We can go to Puna when we finish making the toys."

So they proceeded with the work, making little wooden birds that would float on the waves. They built a toy canoe which they colored red, and made little toy men to paddle it. They carved small idols to stand upright in the canoe and stained these red and black. They folded vine leaves to make *kō'ie'ie* toys which would skip and dance over the water. And last of all they put together a kite, brilliantly colored, one that would climb high into the sky.

Then with playthings and provisions lashed into their own canoe, Hale-mano and his sister got ready to shove off for Puna. Just before they left, Hale-mano's father presented him with a long and finely finished spear tipped with bone, and his mother threw over his broad shoulders a cape fit for a chieftain and hung round his neck a *palaoa*, a talisman carved from the tooth of some great sea animal. The prospects for the voyage were very good, with cloud banks sitting together peacefully in the northwest and the listless winging of the seabirds showing them the favoring wind.

Then, amidst a chorus of *alohas!* the canoe dashed through the breakers and out into the open sea. Hale-mano's high adventure had begun!

After two days of smooth sailing they stood off the eastern cape of Puna, near Ka-poho.

"The wind is steady here," said Laenihi. "Now is the time to take in the sail and put up the kite, so it can be seen by the people in the bay where your princess lives."

While she paddled, Hale-mano let the kite rise high into the air, and soon enough the people on the beach saw it and began to point and shout. They had never seen a kite before. Kama's little brother, Kumu-kahi, heard the noise and ran down to see for himself what was happening. By now Laenihi had steered the canoe 'round the point and into the bay.

"There is her brother," Laenihi said as they spotted a small boy wading out toward them. They paddled closer.

The boy stretched out his hands and started calling to them, "Let me have the thing that flies!"

Laenihi said to her brother, "Yes, let him have the kite."

And Hale-mano put the string of the kite into the boy's hand.

Kumu-kahi let out a happy squeal as he felt the tug. Then he waded back in to shore and ran along the beach with the kite, while all the people cheered.

Before too long, Laenihi took out the toy birds and put them into the water and they floated on the waves. Next, the small canoe was let down where the gentle wind would blow it in through the surf toward the beach. Kumu-kahi saw these new things and wanted to play with them as well. He handed the kite string to a friend and waded out into the water again.

He cried eagerly, "Oh, let me have these things!"

And Laenihi said, "They are for you." And she laughed to see the youngster so delighted.

Kumu-kahi played with his new treasures for a long time at the water's edge, while Hale-mano and his sister waited patiently. Then they brought out the small carved idols and set them up inside their canoe. The boy saw these as well and splashed out to get them, but this time Hale-mano held on firmly to the red and black figures.

Laenihi asked, "Is your sister fond of you?"

"Yes, she is," said Kumu-kahi. "She will do anything I ask her to do. She is really nice to me."

"We will let you have these, too, if you bring your sister to meet us."

The boy waded back in and ran for home with the toy canoe in his hand. He called to his sister, "Kama, come down to the beach with me! Some people are giving away good things—look at this canoe! They have more, but I can't get it from them unless you come along and help me!"

Kama took her brother's hand, and they ran back to the beach together.

In the bright sunlight Hale-mano saw that this was the girl who came to visit him in his dreams! And Kama must have recognized something about Hale-mano as well, because she stopped and looked at him for a long time.

"Come on!" shouted Kumu-kahi, "let's get these toys!" And he pulled her eagerly out into the water.

When they reached the canoe, Hale-mano handed them the little carved idols and at the same time offered to take them on a surf ride back to the beach in his canoe, as some beautiful waves were approaching just then.

Kama and her brother could not resist this opportunity for an exciting ride, so they quickly climbed aboard. The canoe was paddled a short way out beyond the break, where it remained for a moment waiting for a high climbing roller to take them into shore.

One wave passed and was missed and, before the next one came, a squall, or what was called a *mukumuku*, suddenly struck their canoe, rendering it utterly unmanageable and driving it out upon the broad ocean.

Laenihi said, "Look back there on the beach!"

People were running into the water and starting to swim out toward them. Some were launching canoes.

Kama began to cry. "They know I shouldn't be out here with you. They know you're not the king of Puna or the king of Hilo."

They had no time to answer her; it was all they could do to run before the squall.

But after some anxious times, the wild winds slackened to a steady breeze and they were able to put up the sail. Driven as well by the power of Laenihi's magic, their canoe slipped across the sea with the swiftness of an arrow, leaving the angry people far behind.

While the drums were throbbing and the alarm fires began to flare up back on shore, Princess Kama, wrapped in the folds of a soft *tapa*, sat quietly in the canoe and comforted her young brother. But they were far too excited by the strange events of the day to sleep or even try to rest; so they came and sat near Hale-mano in the stern until past midnight, looking out at the curtain of stars and listening to him tell the story of this romantic expedition which began as a dream.

Then Princess Kama confessed that she, too, had seen Hale-mano in her dreams. And when he begged her to look favorably on his proposal of marriage, she frankly replied that, if her brother did not object, she would give the matter her consideration.

The voyagers continued peacefully on their way and soon enough landed back on the island of Oʻahu near the ʻUkoʻa fishpond of Wai-a-lua. When they reached the shore, a crier was sent out to run all around Wai-a-lua and Waiʻanae to tell the people to come and bring presents for Princess Kama. This was the custom called *hoʻokupu*.

About three days after the *hoʻokupu*, Kama said to her young brother,

"I'm sending you back to Puna with some presents for our parents

and our family, so they won't worry too much about us. Tell them that
I am happy and living with good people and that I want to stay here."

Kumu-kahi did not want to leave his sister but he knew he had to
deliver this important message, so sadly he agreed to return to the
island of Hawai'i.

Hale-mano and Princess Kama found nothing to disturb their
desire for each other. When he stopped to look into her eyes, to tell her
how beautiful she was, never before had any words sounded so sweet
to her. When he asked her for a simple flower she twined a fragrant *lei*
for his broad shoulders. And when he asked for a smile, she gave him
her heart.

So it happened in the month of Kaʻaona*, when the crops of the land are always plentiful and the ocean provides the fisherman with his richest harvest, that the marriage agreement of this young couple was made public by a herald.

The bride, beautifully attired and bedecked with flowers, was delivered in all formality to the bridegroom. Then in the evening a delicious *'aha'aina* feast was served to more than a thousand guests, with *hula*, games, and other festivities, including the *mele inoa* songs of the genealogies of both Kama and Hale-mano.

And when the celebrations at Wai-a-lua were over, Kama was carried in a sedan chair by four bearers all the way to Poʻo-amoho village, the ancestral home of Hale-mano. There were almost three hundred people in that train, with several local chiefs as a guard of honor, impressive in their capes and helmets and armed with javelins festooned with flowers and brightly tinted feathers. It was a right royal procession, and its entrance into Poʻo-amoho village set off another round of merrymaking which lasted many more days.

The occasion was a popular theme of song and conversation for generations, all along the Waiʻanae mountain range, and portions of the *mele* recited in welcome of Princess Kama are still remembered.

*May

32

However, back on the island of Hawai'i, the matter was far from settled. When they learned that the princess had been carried off, Hua'a, the king of Puna, and Kulu-kulua, the king of Hilo, were greatly disturbed and got together for a talk.

They said, "Yes, we gave her parents a great deal of nice property with the idea that one or the other of us would marry her. Now it's up to us to find and punish the kidnappers. We have to visit the *kahuna kilokilo* as soon as possible to ask him the proper course of action and what the outcome of this expedition is going to be."

The night that followed was windswept and black, with wild rains coming in from the northwest. Long after sunset the kings entered the outer gate of the *heiau wā i kaua*, the shrine where they made sacrifices to bring them success in war. Their attendants carried a muzzled pig and two geese for this purpose.

By the light of sputtering *kukui* nut torches, the party made its way into the sacred inner courtyard. There they were met by the *kahuna* and a group of junior priests and sorcerers, who received the sacrificial animals and then ordered the attendants out of the compound.

The large *kaikā* drum was then clubbed three times slowly, and the three designated priests came forward with knives in their hands to perform the *'aha* ceremony which would predict the future of the under-takings. They moved with measured pace toward the altar. On either side of them loomed great carved images of Kane, Ku, and Lono, and twenty other less powerful deities.

At the point of sacrifice the *kahuna* chanted a prayer to Hika Po Loa, the Supreme Being, while the assisting priests made separate supplications to each of the idols. Next, the animals were killed and, when they stopped moving, the bodies were placed upon the altar, opened, and carefully examined.

Having completed his inspection, the *kahuna* stepped back.

"Well," asked the kings anxiously, "what do the gods have to say?"

The *kahuna* replied, "The kings of Hilo and Puna will hear it from the oracle now."

Everyone else moved away from the altar so they would not be able to hear. The oracle was hidden by a *tapa* screen at the entrance to the innermost temple, the holiest of holy places, just behind the altar.

All the torches were extinguished, and the *kahuna* disappeared into the intense darkness.

"Speak!" came a voice from inside the sacred chamber.

"Great Power," said the king of Hilo, "give us your blessing. Help us through the dangers which lie ahead."

"Do homage to Kuka'ili-moku. Make glad the war god of your ancestors!" said the voice behind the screen.

"So do I promise," said Kulu-kulua, the king of Hilo.

"So do I promise," said Hua'a, the king of Puna, "but will that give us the victory?"

"Victory!" was repeated by the oracle.

"But where shall we find the princess? Has she been taken to Kaua'i?"

Silence from the oracle.

"To Maui?"

More silence.

"To Moloka'i? To Lana'i?"

Still more silence.

"Is she then on O'ahu?"

"On O'ahu!" came the reply from deep inside the temple.

The kings of Hilo and Puna turned toward each other in high anticipation.

"To O'ahu!" they shouted. "To war! To victory!"

As soon as the general plan of action was agreed upon, the two kings sent messengers out to the districts and villages of eastern Hawai'i to tell the local chiefs of the numbers of men needed for the war party. As weapons were always kept in readiness, they quickly collected an army of two thousand men to sail in a fleet of four hundred canoes of all sizes.

The fighters camped around their chiefs in huts covered with coconut, or *ti* leaves along the shoreline of Puna, while Hilo Bay was fringed with canoes, many of the larger ones painted red and flying gaudy pennants of stout *tapa*. The men brought daggers of wood or ivory, and knives of sharply broken flint and sharks' teeth. They had stone adzes, axes, hatchets and hammers; they had javelins and spears with points of seasoned wood hard enough to splinter bone. Among them were chiefs in yellow capes and helmets, and warriors armed with clubs and slings.

Since plundering was not to be allowed, they brought with them in extra canoes provisions of large quantities of dried fish, coconuts, potatoes, *taro*, live pigs and chickens, calabashes of water, and *kukui* nuts for torches.

They also took along rolls of *tapa* and *lau hala* matting, shell necklaces, ivory, capes, tools, ornaments, and extra weapons to be bartered for whatever supplies they might need from time to time.

At the auspicious hour, the armies of Puna and Hilo set sail for the island of O'ahu. The expedition would have only the month of Ka'aona to find the Princess Kama and bring her back because, from the beginning of the following month, Hinaia'ele'ele, until the end of the year, all warmaking was *kapu*—forbidden by tradition.

But now the bay was swarming with the fleet of war canoes. In one of the largest double canoes rode the *kahuna kilokilo*, the priest who scanned the skies for omens. His body was bent with time, and his hair, white as foam, covered his shoulders like a cloak. The skin was tightly drawn over his parched cheekbones, and his fiercely glistening black eyes gave him the look of a man who dealt with things to be feared. He was surrounded by magical charms and images, and he kept a sand-filled calabash before him with a fire burning in it continually, into which he threw handfuls of gums and oily mixtures spewing forth clouds of incense. His canoe led those of the kings of Hilo and Puna, each with their own priests and figures of war gods, and each flying a red pennant from the masthead. As the fleet swept out into the ocean with a thousand paddles in the water and a thousand spears in the air, the *kahuna kilokilo* jumped up and began a wild war chant which was taken up by the following canoes and carried far across the waves.

Later that evening a council of war was held on board the canoe of the king of Hilo, attended by the king of Puna and the high *kahuna*.

The king of Hilo said, "The chiefs of O'ahu often act together, and a war with one of them may lead to a conflict with the whole island. Our spears are as long as theirs and our knives as sharp, but their numbers may become far too large if our actions are too hasty. As we land we must make them understand that our mission is one of justice and not of conquest. In this way we should be able to get what we want without having to fight every step of the way."

The king of Puna turned to the *kahuna*. "What are our chances?"

The priest replied, "These are the signs: When the sun rises tomorrow, if a thick fog comes from the east, you will be able to persuade the chiefs of O'ahu to see things your way; but if we have clear and hot weather until we reach land, O'ahu will come against you. Now the second sign to watch for is that, if we run into heavy rains and keep sighting rainbows all the way, you will win no matter how heavy the battle."

After these words from the *kahuna*, the canoes once again turned their prows toward O'ahu. The fleet came through nothing but heavy rainfall the rest of the voyage. And when the black storm clouds parted a little to let down strong shafts of sunlight to the sea, brilliant rainbows were displayed there on curtains of mist, giving them the sure sign of victory.

By the dark of the moon they made their landing on the beach of Moku-le'ia just to the west of Wai-a-lua without any alarm being raised against them. The warriors immediately pushed hard inland to reach Po'o-amoho village, the home of Hale-mano, seven miles away. The people they met had no chance to prepare for battle, so they gave way at every point and allowed the armies to pass through. Runners went out to the chiefs of O'ahu to make it known that this was an expedition in pursuit of lawbreakers, not one of conquest.

The sun was just edging up as the war party came over the slope above the village. First the ridge line bristled with spears, then down the hillsides swept the swarms of armed men. In their rapid descent they seemed to be hopelessly scattered, but they re-formed on reaching the valley floor and in good order moved across the narrow stream beside Po'o-amoho. The wildest excitement took hold in the village. Some people ran for their weapons, others ran toward Wai-a-lua and the sea. Then the attack opened with a fierce rush of Kulu-kulua's forces armed with daggers, clubs, and stone axes. They scrambled high over the rough stone walls into the village, and desperate hand-to-hand fighting broke out.

Amidst the screaming and confusion, Hale-mano was quickly able to grab Kama and his grandmother as well; and the three of them rushed to make their escape along a well-hidden trail where they ran for their lives over the tangled roots and vines, foot-eating rocks and fallen branches of the forest floor, headlong in the direction of the Kolekole stream which they hoped to follow back into the uplands.

Finding it and picking their way between its red banks, they climbed upstream frantically for hours before daring to pause, breathing hard with the heat. As they looked far down behind them at their village, they saw one of the larger houses come crashing down in a billow of orange flames and oily black smoke. All resistance had ended in Po'o-amoho, with many dead and very few prisoners.

They knew there was no safety to be had anywhere near, so they kept going all that night and many nights after, their stomachs pinched with hunger, over the ridges and to the shoreline, past Wai-a-lua, up around to Lā'ie Bay on the windward side, then down by Hau'ula, Kua-loa, Kaha-lu'u and Moe-lana.

At Moe-lana, in the damp region of Kekele at the foot of Nu'u-anu Pali, there was a large field of 'awa plants growing. Hale-mano's grandmother, whose name was Ka'ae'ali'i, broke off many of these 'awa branches and they hid themselves under them.

In the meantime the kings of Hilo and Puna had come to an agreement with the chiefs of Oʻahu, and they offered a bounty over the whole island that Hale-mano should be killed on sight and the Princess Kama taken alive. And the people of the Koʻolau, the windward mountain range, got together and searched for them everywhere, even in the ʻawa field of Moe-lana. But they lay well hidden under the glistening leaves Kaʻaeʻaliʻi had covered them with.

Hearts pounding, they listened while the terrifying sounds of the search party drew closer and closer to them, but then turned away and faded slowly in the distance. Still they waited until well after nightfall to come out of hiding. Then they made their cautious way to Kukui, near the shoreline between Wai-mānalo and Maka-puʻu, because they had relatives living there. Their strength was almost gone; they were exhausted by strain and trouble. This family was going to be their last desperate hope.

From the depths of the night they came near the house silently. Hale-mano and Kama lay low while Grandmother went in to talk with the family first. Right away she got a friendly and hospitable welcome, and was told to make herself at home and to make herself comfortable. Then she mentioned Hale-mano and Kama to them and told of the hard traveling they had all been doing.

"Tell them to come in too. We have a young piglet and a nice bed of charcoal to turn him over, a big bowl of sour *poi*, anything you want."

So a delicious meal was prepared in the middle of the night, and this was the first hot food the refugees had tasted in more than a week. Then they all talked peacefully together about times gone by until well into the early morning, when at last Hale-mano let them know how bad things really were.

"There's no turning back now. They will kill us all if they find out that you are hiding me here. Kama and I have to get away from this island. Would you take us over to Moloka'i?"

"The weather is going to be bad, but it will be just as bad for anybody who tries to come after us. We had better take you right now."

They climbed aboard a long black seagoing canoe and stroked it rapidly away from the coastline; but just a short way out, the Moloka'i channel turned into a surging fury as a powerful storm rumbled down over them. Their canoe was pitched from one gigantic wave to another like a little cockleshell. The driving spray stung them hard, pelting their eyes and stealing the breath from them. Their steersman gave everything he had to keep the boat squarely before the whistling and roaring wind, while the rest were kept bailing heavily between emergencies. A less hardy canoe would have stove to pieces, but theirs had been hewn from the trunk of a mighty *koa* tree so it plowed heartily across the raging mountains of water.

Late the next afternoon the wind left them at last and the clouds broke wide open. They found they were beyond the sight of any land, so they tried to keep the canoe pointed into the groundswell. And even though there was not much wind to help their progress, the sea remained rough and restless.

They could make only slight headway toward a distant cloud bank they took to be a sign of land and, when they were again overtaken by the dark of evening, they were completely undecided as to which way to go. The storm might have already carried them hundreds of miles out into the immense ocean.

Their supply of *poi* had been lost during the gale when its container broke loose and was swept overboard, but they still had small portions of dried fish, sweet potatoes, bananas, and a calabash of drinking water. They ate their evening meal cheerfully, as if their stores were endless. This food was especially delicious to Hale-mano because of the loving way Kama offered it to him. Driven from their home, their friends and relations hunted and killed, pitching aimlessly in the midst of the sea with many sharks below, near the end of their provisions—all these misfortunes faded from their minds for a little while as they drew their strength from the love they shared with one another. Hale-mano considered himself a lucky man.

And lucky they were indeed for the first light of dawn showed them they had been drifting close to the shores of Maui, just off the coast of the district of Lele, now called Lahaina. And this was supremely good fortune because in this very place was a *pu'uhonua*, a city of refuge, secure from any and all pursuers, and under the protection of the deity of that spot. If any warrior should come over the high stone walls with the idea of harming anyone inside, the priest-in-charge could have him killed. This place would be a haven of safety for them until the following

month, Hinaia'ele'ele, when all warfare would be *kapu* until the end of the year. The armies of Hilo and Puna would then have to give up their search and go home empty-handed.

After many warm expressions of thanks Hale-mano and Kama went ashore into the city of refuge, and their relatives turned back to O'ahu with the canoe. At long last the young couple would be able to get some rest.

While staying in Lele, they looked up one morning and saw in the distance the top of majestic Mount Hale-a-ka-lā, which seemed to be floating above the clouds. This sight was so appealing to them they were filled with the desire to travel there and perhaps look for a place to settle down and begin a new life. So when it was safe for them to leave, they made their way eastward over the high plains of Kula, then down through the breadfruit groves of 'Ulu-pala-kua, and from there around the rocky cliffs of the southern coast into the lush valley of Kau-pō.

They decided to make their living there among the friendly people who looked unusual to them because of their *'ehu*, reddish hair and warm red complexions. These people must have come from a far island, and they kept pretty much to themselves in Kau-pō; but they made Hale-mano and Kama feel quite welcome and helped them build their house.

They journeyed up the mountainside and picked out the straightest trees, felled them with axes, and brought them down as house timber. They jointed the house posts and the roof beams to fit each other. The corner posts were planted firmly into the ground and lined up with a measuring cord so as to stand at equal height. Next the plate of the frame was laid on the top of the posts from one corner to the other. Tall posts were then set up at each end of the house and the ridgepole lashed between them. Next came supporting uprights and rafters, then the *pili* grass thatching was put on, and finally they made a sliding door. After completing the house, they put up the surrounding fence. Then it was time for a celebration!

They sent for the *kahuna pule* to offer the prayer at the ceremony of trimming the thatch over the door. This prayer was called the *pule kuwa* and, when it had been recited, Hale-mano and Kama were free to occupy their home. They gathered together a big feast for everyone who had worked on the house, and they served steam-roasted hog, chicken, fish, and many sweet delicacies made with sugar cane, bananas, and coconut pudding. Everyone ate until they were tired!

Their new friends gave them many bowls and dishes for the new house and they helped Kama make *lau hala* matting for the floor coverings. So they had their privacy and shelter from the rain and cold, from sun and the scorching heat. But their work was just beginning because, if they were going to have a steady supply of food, they were going to have to plant and maintain a wet patch for the *taro* from which their *poi* would be made.

Banks of earth were first dug up to form the borders of the patch, then beaten hard. Then water was let in from the stream nearby. When this had nearly dried, the four banks were then reinforced with stones, coconut branches, and sugar cane leaves until they were watertight. Then the soil in the patch was broken up, water let in again, and the earth was well mixed and trampled with the feet. A line was then stretched to mark the rows, after which the *huli*, or *taro* tops, were planted in the rows. Every day then, this patch had to be weeded and watered until the *taro* had grown to good size. After about twelve months, it would be mature and ready for pulling, chopping, cooking, and pounding into food.

They also grew sweet potatoes, and had twenty or so coconut trees of old growth and also enough bananas for their everyday use. After a while they added pigs and poultry and brought in some young breadfruit trees. And every few weeks they went down to the sea cliffs and came back with fish, crabs, limpets, and edible seaweeds.

Their life in Kau-pō was therefore very simple and very hard, and Princess Kama was just not accustomed to these ways. She often silently wished to be back among the luxuries she had always enjoyed in Puna. She was always reluctant to return home from their visits to the water's edge.

Kama yearned for the sea; for the exciting surf which had been the sport of her childhood; for those wild white-backed animals of the ocean which she had so easily mounted and ridden to shore; for the rolling thunder of the breakers against the jagged lava cliffs; for the gurgling, whispering murmur of the little wavelets timidly creeping up the beach to kiss and cool her feet. The more she dreamed of the old days, the more desperate she became with her life of poverty and the slime of the *taro* patch back in Kau-pō.

Aware of Kama's passion for the ocean, Hale-mano tried to give her every opportunity to get away from farm life so that her spirit would not be broken. Thus many times he would return alone to work in Kau-pō valley, giving her an extra day or two to enjoy the waves.

Kama would stow her surfboard in their canoe and go paddling outside the cliffs and jagged lava fingers of the coastline, looking for the high-powered swells that came in from the south. On one of these occasions she was heading back from a day of good rides when she came around a point, and there on the beach she saw bright red canoes—the fleet of a king!

The sandy cove was thronged with dancers and musicians and spectators, all enjoying themselves under the shade of the *hala* and coconut trees, with a chief himself as master of ceremonies and the center of attraction. On his head was a helmet adorned with white and scarlet plumes, and from his broad shoulders hung a cape of yellow *'ō'ō* feathers such as only an *ali'i* was permitted to wear. Around his loins was fastened a king's *malo*, and an ivory clasp ornamented his necklace strung with rare and beautiful shells. All eyes were on him as he strolled down the beach toward Kama's canoe. Graciously he greeted the startled princess and made her an invitation to the festivities, which she immediately accepted.

Her limbs and shoulders were bare, and her hair, braided and bound loosely back, was still wet, and grew chilling in the wind where it fell. So Hua'a, the king of Puna, ordered one of his attendants to bring over a covered calabash. The king reached in and pulled out a handsome *kihei*, or mantle, and wrapped it around her shoulders. Then he seated her in the shelter of his own robust form. She smiled her thanks in return for this delicate display of attention, and King Hua'a was forced to admit to himself that all the reports of Kama's great beauty had not been exaggerated; he could not remember a better-looking woman.

A brilliant entertainment of feasting, music and dancing in honor of the lovely stranger followed in the evening, while the king was favored with her companionship. Kama told Hua'a that she had parted from her husband and that she was thinking of going back to Puna before this meeting had happened.

The next morning the well-equipped canoes of the king were taken to the waterline and their expert crews, trained to work the sail and oar together, made everything ready. And in his enormous scarlet double canoe, its masthead flying the pennant of the *'aha-ali'i*, King Hua'a with his twenty paddlers and attendants set sail for Puna, carrying Princess Kama away with them.

Just at this time Hale-mano was coming along the high narrow trail on the ridge above the cove, looking for Kama, and he stopped to watch as the fleet pulled away. When he saw his wife in the lead canoe he broke into a desperate run down the steep path to the beach, jumping down by every short way he could find. Suddenly he lost his footing on some loose gravel and shot down the hillside out of control and landed with tremendous force on a rock ledge some distance below.

Far to the west on the island of Kaua'i, Hale-mano's sisters were surf-riding. When the kings of Hilo and Puna had attacked their village, the parents of Hale-mano and his brothers and sisters all had escaped, finally reaching the island of Kaua'i. Laenihi and her younger sister, Pulee, had gone to stay at Makaīwa because they loved the surf there. This beach was on the leeward side of Kēwā.

As they were surfing, Laenihi began to feel a premonition of some disaster. She looked up into the blue sky and saw the shadow of Hale-mano sitting there. She began to cry because she deeply loved her brother.

She paddled over to Pulee and told her, "Hale-mano is dead."

And later, when their whole family heard of Hale-mano's fate, they all began to weep and mourn.

But Laenihi calmed them by saying, "Don't cry now. Let me pray to the Gods and, if they have any good will for us, Hale-mano will come back to life. If they have no mercy for us at this time, then Hale-mano is on the path of no return. But while I am praying, you must keep still and try to be patient."

When they heard this, they stopped their loud weeping and mourning.

Laenihi turned her face to the blue sky where she again saw the spirit of her brother, and this was her prayer:

> *I sit and cry for you my brother*
> *Hale-mano of the deep forest;*
> *Maybe that is your spirit in the shadows of death,*
> *Piloting the high pointed clouds*
> *Through the hidden reefs of the sky.*
> *Oh, how I cry for you, my beloved.*
> *You are my navigator in the eight island seas.*
> *Come back to me, your friend.*
> *Come back to life;*
> *Come to the feast, put on your best malo;*
> *You are whole again.*
> *You are home!*

And with this prayer, Laenihi was able to bring the life force back into the body of her brother, even though she was on Kaua'i and Hale-mano was on Maui. This was the greatness of her power. Next she plunged into the ocean and changed herself into her fish form, then swam very swiftly toward her brother's island. In a very short time she made the crossing and came ashore, where she found Hale-mano resting, and she fell upon him and wept. She stayed with him for ten days afterwards.

Toward the end of this time, Hale-mano said to his sister, "I'm going to learn how to farm and fish well, so that Kama will have more respect for me and want to come back here to live with me again."

"If that is the way you are going to spend your time, your wife will never come back to you. She is a princess, and her husband must not do ordinary work but something that brings them near the families and friends of the chieftains."

Hale-mano thought of some other crafts he might take up, but each time Laenihi rejected his idea.

Finally he decided he would study the art of singing and chanting, and his sister was delighted.

"That's the skill which will bring your wife back to you; yes, that's it! Can't you see, your name Hale-mano means 'many houses' and, if you become a masterful chanter of people's name-songs and genealogies, you will be invited into every important person's house from Hawai'i to Ni'ihau. A princess would want to stay with a man who passes his days and nights this way, moving here and there and being royally entertained. Answer the call, Hale-mano, you have found your life's work at last!"

So having come to this decision, Laenihi and Hale-mano fondly parted company once again, she to return to her water sports and healing arts and he to make the voyage to Kohala, the northwestern district of the island of Hawai'i, to study singing and chanting. There he entered the *hula halau* of the great teacher La'amai-Kahiki. In this house the *hula* was taught to young, fine looking girls who were good dancers; musicians gained knowledge of their instruments; and the singers polished the many points of their craft. While they were students, no one was allowed to leave the *hula halau*; it was *kapu*, and they could have contact with no one outside. Everyone practiced for a long time every day, with lessons from sunrise until noon and rehearsals until dark. Their food and behavior were strictly watched over, for the whole period of training and performance was considered sacred.

During these years Hale-mano perfected the difficult art of chanting in all its aspects. He learned the traditional songs of war; the genealogies and exploits of the famous chiefs and legendary heroes of Hawai'i; songs of praise; lyrical ballads; name-songs in praise of people of accomplishment; dirges and laments; prayers; satirical and comical songs making fun of the foolish folk; even songs for contests and to comment on fashions of clothing. He also gained a great knowledge of traditions and place names, as well as names for winds, rain and surf. He polished his memory to a keen edge, for a lapse or a wrong word in any performance would be a bad omen. Above all, he gained the understanding of *kaona*, the power of the inner meaning of words.

All these skills came easily to Hale-mano, and his performances gained in power and respectability daily. But the songs which were dearest to his heart, and which were destined to spread his fame all around the Islands, were the songs of love that he composed and sang, always with Princess Kama in mind although he never mentioned her by name.

During all this time, Princess Kama had been living in the royal mansion of King Hua'a in Puna. His was a large home, well over two hundred feet long and very beautifully decorated; and Kama was provided with every comfort and luxury known to the nobility. Her apartments on the terrace had been especially prepared to please her tastes, and there were women in attendance to serve her every need and to see to it that there was nothing she lacked—except, of course, the freedom to come and go. The large private room of her three apartments was filled with all the finest furnishings, most of which had been carried away as unwilling contributions from the less warlike districts of O'ahu and Hawai'i by the soldiers of King Hua'a. The walls were covered with finely woven and brilliantly colored matting, festooned with shining sea shells. The beams of the ceiling were also studded with bright shells and stained in vivid shades of red and orange.

On one side of the room was a slightly raised platform, comfortably padded with sea grass and covered over with many folds of *tapa*. This was her sleeping couch. Over on the other side was a *tapa*-covered lounge which stretched the entire length of the room. And in the middle of the apartment several thicknesses of woven *lau hala* matting were spread, and there Kama took her meals. Light came in through two small openings just under the eaves and from the doorway when its heavy curtains were drawn aside. In one corner of the room stood a row of shelves holding carved calabashes and drinking vessels as well as ornaments made of shells, ivory, and feathers. In huge calabashes under the shelves was stored every type of clothing Princess Kama could expect to wear on any occasion.

The grounds around the palace were thickly planted with shade and fruit trees from every one of the islands of Hawai'i. In under the trees were quiet walkways and vine covered alcoves for sitting and passing the time of day. Sentries stood watch at every entrance. The entire scene was one of royal power and comfort, certainly all the Princess could ever have dreamed of. The only unsettling things to her were that she was never allowed to go anywhere, particularly not to the surf line, and that from time to time King Hua'a would bring home a new wife or two to increase his retinue, as his fancy dictated.

Some of these women were polite enough to Kama, but most were jealous of her and shut her out of their conversations and pastimes; so she began to feel very lonely for the kind of companionship she once had shared with Hale-mano, even though they had been through such hard times in the past.

After one particularly long session of debauchery at the palace, when everybody including the sentries was completely drunk on 'awa and fast falling asleep, she decided to run away. She dressed in old, worn clothing and streaked her hair with ashes, and tiptoed out onto the trail through the *hala* groves in the early dawn. The king then had so many wives she knew she would scarcely be missed; it had been a good long time since he had shown any great interest in her. His main pursuits seemed to be the acquisition of more property, mistresses, and body weight.

Hale-mano finally completed his education at the *hula halau* and with much ceremony and acclaim was declared an expert at the graduation concert performed before all the nobility of the district of Kohala. After that many people invited him to come into their homes to entertain.

One time he was on his way to an important festival, and he happened to pass by a grove of *'ōhi'a* trees in a place called Ke'a-kui. He saw *maile* vines growing on the trees there, and he went in to strip leaves from these vines to make some *leis* to wear and to give to his hosts. From where he sat down he could easily see clear across the 'Ale-nui-hāhā channel over to the island of Maui, where he could make out the top of Mount Hale-a-ka-lā, looking like a pointed cloud in the evening with other clouds drifting around it. As he watched Mount Hale-a-ka-lā, he

remembered the first time he and his lost love had come across that scene in their travels. And just at the very time he was thinking of her, Princess Kama, who had been wandering all over the island of Hawai'i, happened to enter that same grove where he was sitting.

She saw Hale-mano, and she knew him; she came, and she stood behind him, and she longed to come up and put her hand out to touch him, for he looked very handsome. He was singing to himself in a fine voice:

> "I was once thought a good deal of, O my love!
> My companion of the shady trees.
> For we two once lived on the food from the long-
>   speared grass of the wilderness.
> Alas, O my love!
> My love from the land of Kaumuku wind,
> As it comes gliding over the ocean,
> As it covers the waves of Papa-wai,
> For it was the canoe that brought us here.
> Alas, O my love!
> My love of the home where we were friendless,
> Our only comfort being our love for one another.
> It is hooked, and it bites to the very inside of the
>   bones."

Kama would have put out her hand to touch him but, hearing him sing so sorrowfully, she thought he was too badly hurt ever to forgive her. She turned and moved silently away, her eyes flooding with tears.

At this time Hale-mano was courting Kīkē-ka'ala, who was the daughter of one of the high chiefs of the district of Kohala. Kīkē-ka'ala was a woman of great wealth, if not beauty; and she sent out an order which was carried all over Kohala inviting everyone to come to the Makahiki harvest festival in honor of the God Lono, to be held at Lole-hale. Lole-hale, the most famous place of its day for these celebrations, was situated on a hill looking to the west, close under the summit of Pu'u-onale.

People came from all over Kohala to pay their taxes and to join in the sports, and feasting, and dancing. No farming, no fishing, no religious duties, no work of any kind was allowed during the time of Makahiki which went on for four months beginning with Ikuwa, the season of storms when the seas shout, men and women shout, and there is no one who is not shouting.

People came with pigs, *taro*, sweet potatoes, feathers, *tapa* and mats, and all the things that were made, and they laid them as offerings on the altars of the God Lono. When the king and his followers and the priests had taken their choice, the rest was divided up among the people. Then the festivities began. Every musical instrument was put to use, and for five days in this part of the island there would be a continuous uproar of merrymaking, after which the procession would move on to the next district until the entire island had been circled.

Laka, the Goddess of the *hula*, was brought out and decorated with flowers and feathers; and every kind of dance was given, some of them to the rhythm of vocal recitations, and others to the noisier accompaniment of flutes, drums, and rattling thumping gourds.

In the middle of these enjoyments, long-bearded poets appeared before the king and the distinguished chiefs and, while some of them recited wild historic tales of bygone days, others chanted the *mele inoa*, singing of the personal exploits of their listeners. *'Awa* and other intoxicating drinks flowed freely all during the festival, so that there would be a week of general weakness and worthlessness to follow.

The season of Lono was a time when everyone joined in the games: *pūhenehene*, guessing where the pebble is hidden in the tapa cloth; the game of *ke'a pua*, ricocheting the arrows made from sugar-cane tassels; the game of *pahe'e*, casting the javelin along the grass for distance; juggling, called *pūkaula*; foot racing, known as *kūkini*; wrestling, *hākōkō*; boxing, *mokomoko*; sliding down the hillside course on the *hōlua* sled; finger pulling contests called *ku'i-a-lua*; cockfighting, known as *ho'ohaka-moa*; and rolling the *maika* stone disc. All these activities and many more brought delight and fame to those who were successful, and hope for a better performance at the next festival to those on the losing side.

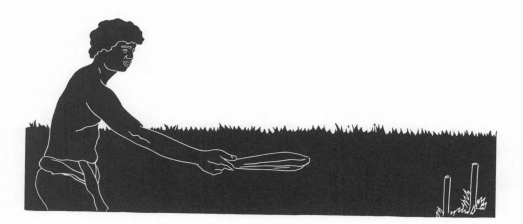

73

Now the pastime which brought Hale-mano to the hill of Lole-hale was the matchmaking game called *kilu*. *Kilu* was an exclusive and aristocratic activity to which only the chiefly *ali'i* were admitted. However, once allowed inside the hall where the sport was held, everyone was considered on an equal footing with regard to the privileges and rules of the game.

The men sat in a group at one end of the hall, the women at the other. Five players of each sex sat facing each other, in front of the spectators, separated by a space of about twelve feet. The floor which lay between the players was covered with *lau hala* matting. The players were selected by the president of the game, who was called the *lā anoano*.

In front of each player was placed a heavy wooden cone, broad at the base so as to stand upright. The *kilu* with which the game was played was a dish made by cutting a coconut shell obliquely in two. The player tried to slide the *kilu* so that it spun across the matting to hit the wooden

block standing in front of the partner of his or her choice. A successful hit entitled the player to claim a kiss from the opponent, and it was customary to demand payment then and there. The successful scoring of ten points entitled one to claim the companionship of the chosen partner. As a practical matter, however, this right was sometimes transformed into a gift of land or some other possession.

After everyone had arrived at the festival of Lono, Hale-mano was requested to chant and participate in the *kilu* game.

The daughter of the chief, Kīkē-kaʻala, said to him: "I will make a little bet with you. If I beat you in the *kilu* throwing, then you will belong to me. And if you beat me, then I will belong to you. What do you think of that idea?"

Hale-mano said, "That sounds like a good bet to me," because he felt the time had come again when he should have a wife; and this game of *kilu* would be a good way of making public the agreement he had already reached with Kīkē-kaʻala.

As soon as everything was ready, the president of the *kilu* game called out, "Pūheoheo!"

And the assembly answered, "Pūheoheo-heo!"

Then all became quiet. The tally keeper on the women's side held up the *kilu* to be thrown by Princess Kīkē-kaʻala, and announced, "If she hits her mark, she gets a kiss from her man!"

Then the game began. Everyone had to chant a few verses from a love song before casting the *kilu*, so Kīkē-kaʻala started by singing,

> "You were thinking me to be a stranger,
> I am myself from crown to sole.
> Hidden has been my love
> Pent up within
> Shown by my weeping over you.
> Now the worm wiggles to its goal.
> What scuffling; a hasty entrance;
> Pinned!
> Down comes the rain!"

Then she slid her first shell over the matting; but it went wide of the mark.

Now it was Hale-mano's turn. As he got ready to throw, he looked over toward Kīkē-ka'ala; but whom should he see behind her in the crowd of onlookers but his own first love, the Princess Kama, sitting there in all her beauty and grace!

His mind flew back to the days of their youth; and when he began his song of love, it was for Kama, for her alone:

> "The sea is hewing down the hala trees of Puna.
> They are standing there like people,
> Like a multitude in the lowlands of Hilo.
> Step by step the sea rises to flood the Isle of Life.
> So life revives within me for love of you.
> For anger is a helper to man,
> As I wandered friendless over the highways
> That way and this way.
> What of me, my love
> Alas, my own dear love
> My companion of the low-hanging breadfruit trees of
>   Kala-pana
> Of the sun rising cold for Kumu-kahi.
> The love of a wife is indeed above everything else
> For my temples are burning and my heart is cold for
>   your love
> And my body is under bonds to this other woman.
> Come back to me, for we are in a strange place
>   together,
> My love, come back,
> Come back and let us warm each other with love
> My only friend in a friendless land."

Hale-mano was telling Kama with this song that he had completely forgiven her. As he played the game of *kilu*, he cast and hit the mark each time, hoping that he might take his choice at the finish and be released from the bet with Princess Kīkē-ka'ala. Ten times he chanted, and ten times he slid the *kilu*, and ten times he hit his mark!

But at the end of the game, Kīkē-ka'ala rushed up to Hale-mano and pulled him toward her, shouting at Princess Kama, "You deserted him and here you are, coming after him again. He is not going to return to you!"

Then Kīkē-ka'ala signaled for a group of her father's strong men to come around Hale-mano and herself and escort them away from the *kilu* hall. And as they started off into the night, Princess Kama was left standing there weeping. She wrung her hands behind her back and, as the tears flowed down her face, she took up a song of her own:

> "This land is burning with fire.
> It is burning with the flame of Goddess Pele,
> It is raging in the uplands of Hāmākua,
> It is being cut up by the wind
> Causing anger and hatred,
> Ill feeling and bad thoughts."

She stopped her singing a little to look lovingly at Hale-mano. When she did, she saw Kīkē-ka'ala biting him on his ear, so she sang out once more.

> "The bite of this woman is a treacherous sign.
> The stranger laughs; it is a sign of evil.
> You are surrounded by fine rain from the goddess.
> I must be your wife and you my husband."

She kept on singing, but soon she was surrounded and forcibly led away by the men of Kīkē-kaʻala's father.

Hale-mano could just barely hear her voice as it grew fainter in the distance:

"The wind is blowing.
It is the woman of a strange land.
You will surely see Haili,
Haili the plain of lehua flowers entwined by the birds.
They are carrying away the 'awa of Puna that grows
     on the trees,
The sweet sounding 'ō'ō bird of the forest
Whose beautiful notes can be heard at eventide.
My companion of the cold watery home outside Hilo
Where you and I first embraced,
My own beloved husband."

At this, Kīkē-ka'ala shouted after her, "You have no husband because you are a woman who deserted her husband. I see that you have come to try to get him away from me; but I shall make sure this will never happen."

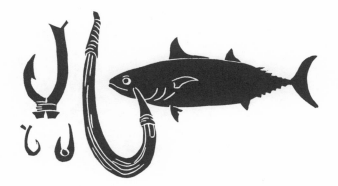

After that night, Hale-mano and Kīkē-ka'ala lived together as husband and wife. She clung to him day and night; wherever he went, she followed until he had had enough.

He was tired and angry from being shut up in the house all the time. Because of this, he said to Kīkē-ka'ala one day, "Say, I hear the *aku*, the tuna, are really running well at the fishing grounds down by Ka'ele-huluhulu. If I start right away, I can bring us back a canoe full. If I don't go now, they will be gone."

Kīkēka'ala said, "It's better if I go with you."

Hale-mano told her, "Your duty is to stay here and observe the *kapu*. My job is to lash the fishhooks, say the prayers, get down to the landing quickly, and head for the fishing grounds—all without talking to anyone. Then I have to watch where the *noio* birds are diving, paddle hard with the current, and throw my lines over the side to catch the *aku* at the surface. It's hard work, and you just can't learn it in a day. I will take you sometime when the fishing is easy. Don't worry, I'll be back in no time."

After a little more arguing, his wife let him go; and Hale-mano hurried away at last. He set out from the cove at Pu'a-wela; but instead of going fishing, he turned the prow of his canoe toward Hāmoa on the island of Maui, where he landed that evening just as the sun was going down.

On the other hand, the Princess Kama started off in a canoe of her own soon after Hale-mano had left the coast of Hawai'i; and she, too, landed at Hāmoa on Maui, where the sea dances, where the surf is always good, and the fishing and the fruit from the trees are always the best.

And there they found each other again. For a moment he gazed on her careworn face; for a moment she marveled at the gray in his hair. He took her hand and held it to his heart, and the silence that followed best revealed the thoughts of both. There were tears in their eyes, but they were tears of happiness.

And so ended their lonely searching, for they lived with each other from then on.

Sprinkled, the tale runs.

Glossary

'aha'aina	Banquet, feast.
aku	Tuna, an important food item.
ali'i	Chieftain, noble (male or female).
'awa	A tall shrub with green, heart-shaped leaves; a ceremonial liquor is prepared from its roots.
'ehu	Reddish tinge in hair, of Polynesians and not of Caucasians; reddish-brown complexion said to be characteristic of some *'ehu* people.
hala	Pandanus tree; its long, spine-edged leaves are plaited into mats, baskets, and hats.
hale hau	House built for healing the sick.
heiau wā i kaua	A heiau, or shrine, used for services and where offerings were made to bring success in war.
Hi'i-aka	Goddess of healing; a younger sister of Pele, the fire goddess.
ho'okupu	To broadcast, as in spreading the news or sowing or scattering seeds.
hula halau	Long house for *hula* instruction.
huli	Taro top.
kahuna	Priest, sorcerer, professional expert.
kahuna kilokilo	Priest who watches the skies for omens.
kahuna pule	Priest who blesses the newly built house.
kaika	Cultivated *taro* patch.
kaona	Hidden meaning in Hawaiian poetry; concealed reference, as to a person, thing, or place; words with a double meaning that might bring good or bad fortune.

85

Ka-poho	Village on the east coast of the island of Hawai'i, buried by a lava flow in 1960.
kapu	Taboo, prohibited, sacred.
kapua	The supernatural ability to transform into several forms; magic powers.
Kēwā	Section of land near Wai-lua on the island Kaua'i.
kihei	Shawl, cape, mantle; rectangular tapa garment worn over one shoulder and tied in a knot.
kilu	A small gourd or coconut shell, usually cut lengthwise, used for storing small, choice objects, or used as a quoit in the *kilu* game.
koa	Acacia tree furnishing fine red wood for canoes, surfboards and serving bowls.
ko'ie'ie	A water toy made of plaited leaves.
kukui	Candlenut tree; its white, oily nuts were burned for lamplight.
kupua	A supernatural being capable of assuming several forms—human, pig, fish, etc.
lā anoano	Person presiding over the game of *kilu*.
lau hala	The leaves of the pandanus tree, used for plaited mats, baskets, and hats.
lehua	The tufted flower of the *'ohi'a* tree, most often bright red.
lei	Garland, wreath.
maika	A game similar to lawn bowling.
maile	A twining shrub with shiny, fragrant leaves used for decoration and *leis*.
malo	Loincloth.
mana	Supernatural or divine power; miraculous power.

mele inoa	Chant composed in honor of a notable person.
muku	Short, brief; anything cut off short.
noio	A seabird, the Hawaiian tern.
noni	Indian mulberry, used for making dyes and medicines.
'ōhi'a	Hardwood plant with many forms, from tall trees to low shrubs.
'ō'ō	A black, honey-eating bird.
pā'ū	Woman's skirt, sarong.
pili	Clinging grass, used for thatching houses.
poi	Pudding-like, pasty derivative of the cooked and pounded roots of the *taro* plant; the staple food of the Hawaiians.
pule kuwa	A prayer offered at the ceremony of trimming the thatch over the door of a new house.
Puna	Southeast portion of the island of Hawai'i.
Pūheoheo!	The opening call of the leader of the kissing game of *kilu*; the players answered by calling *Puheoheo-heo!*
Pū'uhonua	Place of refuge, asylum; place of peace and safety.
tapa	(Kapa) made from *wauke* or *mamaki* bark; formerly clothes of any kind, or bedclothes.
taro	Starchy tuberous edible plant cultivated throughout Polynesia.
ti	A woody plant in the lily family; the leaves are used for thatching houses, food wrappers, *hula* skirts; the sweet roots are baked for food or fermented and distilled into liquor.

References

The Legends and Myths of Hawaii
  By His Hawaiian Majesty, King David Kalakaua.
  Published by Charles L. Webster & Co., New York, 1888.

Ancient Hawaiian Civilization
  A series of lectures delivered at the Kamehameha Schools, 1933, by
  Handy, Emory, Bryan, Buck, Wise, and others.
  Published by Charles E. Tuttle Co., Inc. of Rutland, Vermont, and
  Tokyo, Japan, 1965.

Moolelo of Ancient Hawaii
  By the Reverend John F. Pogue, 1858.
  Translated from Hawaiian by Charles W. Kenn.
  Published by Topgallant Publishing Co., Ltd., Honolulu, 1978.

Fragments of Hawaiian History
  By John Papa Ii (1866–1870). Translated by Mary Kawena Pukui.
  Published by Bernice P. Bishop Museum Press, Honolulu, 1959.

Hawaiian Antiquities (Moolelo Hawaii)
  By David Malo.
  Translated by Nathanial B. Emerson (1898).
  Published by Bernice P. Bishop Museum, Special Publication 2,
  Honolulu, 1971.

Arts and Crafts of Hawaii
    By Te Rangi Hiroa (Peter Buck).
    Published by Bernice P. Bishop Museum Press, Honolulu.
    Special Publication, 1957.

Hawaiian Games for Today
    By Donald D. Kilolani Mitchell.
    Published by Kamehameha Schools Press, Honolulu, 1975.

The Seasons of Mahina 1980 (Calendar)
    By Richard P. Wirtz.
    Produced by Graphic Arts and Letters Unlimited, Honolulu, 1980.

Hawaiian-English Dictionary
    By Mary Kawena Pukui and Samuel H. Elbert.
    Published by the University of Hawaii Press, Honolulu, 1957.

Place Names of Hawaii
    By Mary Kawena Pukui, Samuel H. Elbert & Esther T. Mookini.
    Published by the University Press of Hawaii, Honolulu, 1974.

Reference Maps of the Islands of Hawai'i
    By James A. Bier. O'ahu 1977, Hawai'i 1976, and Maui 1976.
    Published by the University Press of Hawaii, Honolulu.

Sources

Legend of Hale-mano
   in Abraham Fornander's
   Hawaiian Antiquities and Folk-Lore, Vols. 4 & 5.
   Published by the Bernice P. Bishop Museum Memoirs, Honolulu,
   1919.

The Story of Hale-mano and the Princess Kama
   In Padraic Colum's
   At the Gateways of the Day.
   Published by Yale University Press, New Haven, 1924.

Hale-mano and the Princess Kama
   In Eric A. Knudsen's
   Teller of Hawaiian Tales.
   Copyright W. H. Male, Honolulu, 1945.

Hale-mano
   In Martha Warren Beckwith's translation of
   The Hawaiian Romance of Laieikawai by S. N. Haleole, 1863.
   Published by Bureau of American Ethnology Annual Report 33 (for
   1911–1912), Washington, D.C.

A Kite and a Toy Canoe
   in Mary Kawena Pukui's
   Pikoi and Other Legends of the Island of Hawaii.
   Published by Kamehameha Schools Press, Honolulu, 1949.